Pal the Pony

Sal to the Rescue

by R. A. Herman
illustrated by Betina Ogden

SCHOLASTIC INC.
New York Toronto London Auckland Sydney
Mexico City New Delhi Hong Kong Buenos Aires

To Gabriel, who likes ponies
— R.A.H.

For Paris . . .
— B.O.

ISBN 0-439-57745-4

Text copyright © 2003 by R. A. Herman.
Illustrations copyright © 2003 by Betina Ogden.
All rights reserved. Published by Scholastic Inc.
SCHOLASTIC and associated logos are trademarks and/or registered trademarks of Scholastic Inc.

12 11 10 9 8 7 6 5 4   3 4 5 6 7 8/0

Printed in the U.S.A.
First printing, October 2003

It is a beautiful fall day on the Star Ranch.
Pal and Sal are in the field.

The cool breeze blows Pal's mane.
Pal feels so good. He wants to run.

"Come on, Sal," he calls. "Let's run and run and run."
And off he goes. He does not wait for Sal.

He runs through the field of tall grass.

He runs past the pond.

He jumps over the fallen tree.

He runs up the hill . . .

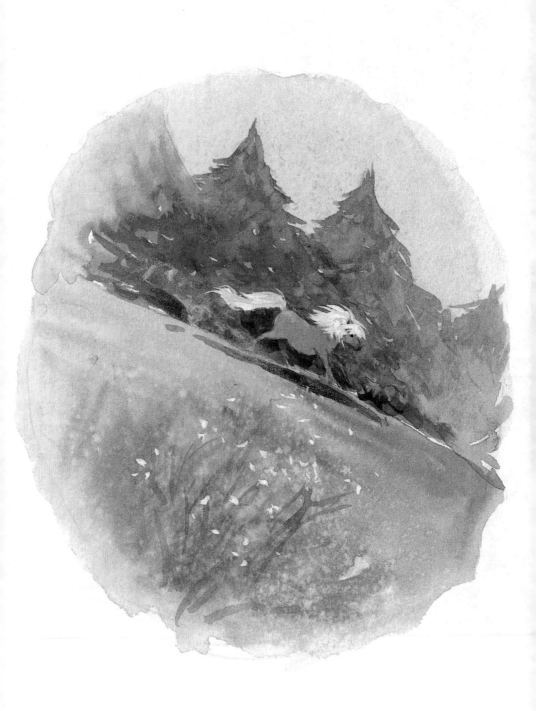

. . . and then down the other side.

Pal runs and runs and runs until he comes to the woods.

He stops and asks, "Wasn't that fun, Sal?"

Sal does not answer.
Pal turns around to look for her.

Sal is not there.
Pal calls for her. "Neigh! Neigh!"

But there is no answer. Where is Sal?

Pal is tired and hungry after all that running.

So he nibbles some grass and swishes his tail.

Nibble, nibble. Swish, swish.

The sun sets. The sky gets dark.
Pal wants to go back to the ranch.

He starts to walk, but he does not know which way to go.

"Hoot! Hoot!"
What is that sound? Pal wonders.
Pal is scared.

He really wants to be home,
safe in the barn.

He calls again. "Neigh! Neigh!"

This means, "I am lost."

Pal feels like crying.
But he hears "Neeeigh!"

And there is Sal.

Pal is so happy to see her.

"Pal," says Sal. "Next time, wait for me."

"Oh, I will," says Pal. "Do you know how
to get back to the ranch?"
"Yes. Follow me," Sal says.

They trot up the big hill . . .

. . . and down the other side.

They jump over the fallen tree.

They walk around the pond.
Pal and Sal are too tired to trot anymore.

They walk through the field of tall grass.
Now they can see the lights in the barn.

Pal and Sal are happy to be home in time for dinner.
Nibble, nibble. Swish, swish.